Angela Woodward

End of the Fire Cult

Acknowledgments:

Much of this book was written during a residency at the Kimmel Harding Nelson Center for the Arts. The author thanks the Kimmel Foundation and KHN staff Denise Brady and Pat Friedli. Thanks also to early readers Susan D'Amato, Amy Schapiro, Ushio Torikai, Gwen Walstrand, Mickle Maher, and Lisa Black, and to Robert Jacobson, Isabel and Abner.

"Intellectual Property," "Commerce," "Literature I," "Enhanced Distribution" and "Fertility" appeared previously in *Ninth Letter.*

Cover Design: Andrea Trum

First Edition
ISBN: 978-0-9822115-8-8
LCCN: 2010937100

Ravenna Press
Spokane, Washington, USA
www.ravennapress.com

Also by Angela Woodward:

The Human Mind

(Ravenna Press)

End of the Fire Cult

Angela Woodward

Mamma & Daddy,

Thanks for your enthusiasm.

Angela

11-10-10

INTELLECTUAL PROPERTY

Three years ago my husband gave me two-thirds of an exceptionally beautiful and sacred mountain. I disputed whether he owned it in the first place, but I accepted through treaty his offer of the majority portion. The mountain lay on the northern border of a country I had intricately imagined a year earlier. I visualized it at first as a topographical map, hillocks and indentations mostly shrouded in mist. But gradually it became clearer to me, and I filled it with barley fields and tin mines, forests, a few largish towns, and many pleasant hamlets. I gave it a capital city, a system of decaying highways, a library, a river port. I considered placing a benign queen in charge, but then named it the Free Republic of Marmoral, and put it under the auspices of a hereditary oligarchy of thieves. I peopled the towns with several tribes of conflicting religions and a useful urban poor. The countryside remained quiet and green, more of a mystery. I used to tell my husband about it, back when we leaned against each other in the evenings, and sometimes he would ask if he could add a little bit — a touristy waterfall, a rare species of hummingbird. "I don't think that's quite right," I said.

At first I thought all of Marmoral might be high in the mountains, the air thin and piercing, almost unbreathable to outsiders. But that began to seem trite to me, too toylike. I wanted something more graspable. Unfortunately, by the time I had imagined the holy mountain on the northern border, my husband had laid claim to his own land. His country, Belgrave, straddled the mountain and then sprawled off into a chain of foothills beyond. But because his country's rulers were a long-standing warlike people, he told me they had seized the mountain in its entirety some three thousand years before I came on the scene. My people, he said, could gaze at the heights on clear days. Every August 11 we could climb to the temple in the grotto and drink a special holiday herbal tea. But for the rest of the year, we were not to set foot on it. His government policed the border fence vigilantly, and practiced target shooting on Marmolian goats that strayed over.

For weeks I cried and begged, and then I began to pay attention to a budding aeronautics industry in the central district. After work, after supper, I lay back in my chair, eyes fixed on the cobwebs on the wall, and imagined a few Marmolians educated abroad, who returned to start a commercial jet factory in a town known before only for apples and dark beer. My husband spent his time at the kitchen table, perhaps looking for inspiration for his country from the swirls in the formica. He finally made a peace offering. Not half but two-thirds of the holy mountain would belong to Marmoral. All he asked was the loan of some of my engineers, and that I would help him maintain good relations with the vast country to our south.

I knew nothing about this other place. It cropped up overnight. Everything was new there, torn down every couple years and built again, the door handles on the squalid high-rises polished, the street lights a hideous burning blue, the trains eerily silent and fast. These southerners bought a fleet of Marmoral airplanes, but then reverse engineered them and made their own. They poured acids down the rivers and dumped infected sheep carcasses over the border. They began making demands—their cigarettes should be stocked in our corner markets, our corner markets should be bought up by their grocery chain, we should watch their movies and educational newscasts, our government of thieves should resign. They didn't bother my husband's country in the same way, maybe because he sent them a steady flow of young women to be nannies, maids, and prostitutes. "It's not fair," I said, as he walked with me to the video store. "What do they want?" He professed he couldn't tell me. My Marmoral was a buffer between his country and the Southern Empire, so it didn't seem to matter to him.

One night he handed me a document claiming mineral rights to the sacred mountain. He had granted me the surface, but not what lay under the ground. He wanted as well a percentage of the proceeds from the restaurants and lodges near the summit, which were always filled to bursting near the August 11 holiday. He also demanded rights to the holiday itself, which his people had inaugurated in their urbanity and wisdom when my people were nothing more than a few families of ignorant herders. The monks in the monastery were to pledge allegiance to Belgrave, which had been their ancestral home before the civil war in the last century. Signs were to be printed in two languages. This was already the case, but he wanted it strictly enforced, with inspections and monetary penalties. "My love," I said. "It was a gift." But I could see by the hard set of his chin that the circumstances had changed.

COMMERCE

I decided to give my husband something to appease him. He had taken back his mountain and its holiday, and bereft as I was, I began to be afraid he would take more. I was ashamed of my weakness. But I couldn't help thinking that Daniel was, if not smarter and stronger than me, clearly more ruthless. I should have remained offended and aggrieved, but instead I offered him a precious commodity, sending a powerful magician into his territory.

The Marmolian magician was a seer. If provided with a pan of flour, he could map the future from the ridges in it. He owned a key that could open any door, and a bag of rose petals that made women fall in love. He was also a thief and a liar, a womanizer and a drunk.

He knocked on the door of a farm on the outskirts of Belgrave's capital. A woman in mourning opened up. It was obvious from her clothes that she was a widow, and from her red-rimmed eyes, her husband's death must have been recent. Two babies yowled in the further room.

The magician pushed his way in, asking for a glass of water. It was bad luck to deny strangers water, and soon he was settled in the kitchen, holding her wrist above the pan she had filled with flour.

"You will have another son within a year," he told her, squinting at the undulations her fingers had left in the grain. He also saw, though he did not tell her, that her husband had hidden gold in the wall.

"How could I have a child?" she said wonderingly, as if the process was new to her. She picked up the littler baby, and it lifted her shirt and clamped its mouth to her nipple. The magician watched a stain bloom on the other side of her shirt as milk spurted from the opposite breast.

"I am very tired," he said. "I walked all day, after men stole my horse."

He persuaded her to pour him a glass of wine, while he untied his boots. The older child came closer and stared at him from behind his mother's legs. The magician drank and brooded while the widow made pancakes. It was imperative, he told her, to consume the flour he had divined with, or else something terrible would happen. She beat the batter, singing softly. The magician leaned back in his chair.

When her sisters and uncles came over, he exited quickly, but after dark he crept back in.

"Oh, I'll make you a bed in the kitchen," she said, rising from her mattress. But the magician quietly picked the sleeping children up out of their mother's bed and settled them on the floor. He undressed and slid in beside her. He rolled one of his magic rose petals along her neck and down her sternum. After that, her taut body became more docile.

When the widow had drifted off to sleep, he roused himself to go search for her late husband's gold. He knocked and tapped, then with his magic key, he sketched a door in the thick plaster wall. He twisted the key and the portion of wall swung open. The magician lifted two sacks of coins down and hid them in his knapsack.

When he climbed back in beside the widow, she seized his arm. "Give me a wish," she said. "I know who you are. I couldn't believe my luck that you came." She thought he was a famous Belgrave sorcerer, despite his sing-song Marmoral accent. She wanted to see the face of her dead husband again. And not the corpse's face, she warned. She wanted to glimpse him as he'd looked in life, just once more.

"Don't you see him in dreams?" he asked.

"Yes, but not his face," she said. "It's only been four months, but I can't remember it." The magician had thought her husband was more likely only four days dead, and he wondered. He had no power to create the vision she wanted. Nevertheless, they went out into the dark yard. They knelt over the water trough, the magician mumbling and swishing his hands back and forth. He was tired. He really had walked all day after men stole his horse, and they had kicked him in the ribs too, and stepped on his hand. He asked the widow to bring him more wine. It was the sweet white wine of the border region, with its peculiar moldy flavor from the shrubby herb that grew wild all over these particular hills. It was very much a taste of home for him, though he was in a foreign country. He drained his glass and held his hands steady over the water. The moon was just a tiny sliver in the sky, but the cold stars were out in force. He wondered what had gone wrong with his rose petals, that the widow wasn't in love with him. She shouldn't have given another thought to her husband now that he had touched her with his charm.

As he chanted nonsense syllables, he wondered, too, about the gold. He hadn't looked in the bags, but only stuck them in his knapsack. He thought maybe they were full of chips of pottery. They had clinked and felt heavy, but he hadn't verified. Now he had a suspicion that the widow had tricked him. Pressing against his shoulder but seeming oblivious to him, she breathed heavily as she peered into the water.

"Do you see him?" he asked. The starlight showed him her image. She was holding her dark hair back with one hand as she leaned over. He had almost not noticed the pure oval of her face before. Reflecting up at him, she seemed now incomparably beautiful, like a fairy. Though it had only been half an hour ago, he remembered as if from the distant past a moment in her bed, when she had twisted under him and put her hands on his hips, drawing him deeper in. When he cried out, she put her hand over his mouth so the children wouldn't wake up.

"I see him," she whispered. "There he is!" The magician let out a moan of despair.

"Look at me!" he said. But she folded herself closer over the trough. The magician could see only her ecstatic face, lips parted, shining out of the depths of black water. He picked up a rock and dropped it in. The smooth surface broke into rings, and finally she turned her head to him, eyes lancing violent hatred.

EARLY HISTORY

"Maybe you should come up with your country's early history," said my husband. He had been working furiously over the last few days, but now appeared suspiciously relaxed. "You know, founding, exploration, draining the swamps for the capital, all that."

He must have given his ancient Belgrave a glorious past, the son of a god marching in, killing the evil dragon-dog that had wound its tail all through the foothills, and then inventing fire, written language, and symmetry.

Daniel went back to the kitchen to wash up. Of course I had already done the dishes, but I'd left the pasta pot to soak, and then I'd had some peanuts in a bowl and half a beer, and taken a dirty tea cup out of the bedroom, so though I had cleaned, the kitchen was still or again a mess. He stood up very straight, running the hot water with enormous confidence.

If his people were descended from gods, I had to have another line. I could have made my own glorious creation myth, but I knew it hadn't really happened that way. The Marmolians had always been the weaker ones, their strength in their persistence and adaptability, not their courage. They were grass, even weeds, not lions.

I went to bed early, while Daniel stayed up puttering around, no doubt designing commemorative statuary for Belgrave's shining capital plaza. Meanwhile, on the edge of an itinerant village, a band of hunters came across a mysterious animal. They were experienced woodsmen, and knew every kind of creature, even the rare black fox. But they had never met or heard of this animal before. It was something like an antelope, though with very short horns and a broader chest. Its knees lay crushed up under it in deep snow, and its brown body heaved with effort. It cast huge eyes up at them out of a long, sad face and moaned speakingly. The men ran back to the village to get the shaman. The shaman knew even the animals only mentioned in spirit tales, that were secret from the common people. But he too found this animal strange, like nothing he knew of. Nevertheless, since the animal seemed to want something from them, the shaman encouraged the hunters to approach it. They wrapped their arms around it and heaved it to its feet. The animal shuddered and collapsed again. Three times the men lifted it. Once it took one step forward, but it was evidently too weak to hold its weight, and it kept falling back into the snow.

The shaman promised the hunters that the beast meant them no harm, and they blessed it with their fingers and returned to the village. The next day, snow blew across its open eyes. Summer reduced it to a pile of odd bones, and by that time, the village had relocated to the shores of Lake Gall.

Nine years later, a group of Belgravians rode into the village and arrested the shaman. They read out a document declaring that on that winter day nine years ago he had butchered a calf belonging to one Harold Moxley, and he would be taken to the regional governor's bureau for trial. The document described the calf's markings in detail, including a white patch on its left shoulder in the shape of a dog's hind leg.

The shaman remembered the mark. His hand had lain right over that white patch as he helped prop the animal up, and when they had left it in the snow, the muscles rippled under the hide in its last struggles, making the white patch jerk.

The shaman had never forgotten the encounter with the strange animal. Even when in the next few seasons the Belgravian cattle had become commonplace, even a nuisance, the frequent sight had not relieved this first cow of its mystery and significance. But how remarkable the Belgravian's writing, this alien technology. The foreigners had brought it with them, along with their domesticated animals, and they guarded the secret of its manufacture. Now the black marks on paper conjured the lost calf in all its specificity. And even more powerful still, these ink writhings commanded soldiers to lay the shaman on the block and chop his arms off. Now there was nothing he could grasp, no tool, he couldn't bless or curse, or ward off evil by throwing salt. But in another way, his understanding had enlarged, and grew larger still as the blood ran out of him.

"What kind of founding father is that?" said Daniel the next morning. I zipped up my skirt and went to work.

FIRE 1 – HOPE

In winter, many Marmolians began their holy week with a festival of fire. They built fires in the huge iron pots in all the temples. The priests and acolytes kept them lit all night long, throwing on the sticks of fragrant wood from incense groves in the east, donated by wealthy parishioners. The sharp, resinous smoke filled the capital. In the countryside and small towns, people burned what they could. They threw any kind of timber onto pyres in their yards or alleys, or on the shorn commons. Only right at midnight did they add the hoarded sticks of precious sandalwood. What a smell of home it was, that burst of fragrance. The cinders started up from the fire and twisted meaningfully—to the right, happiness, to the left, disaster. Curling plates of black ash wafted between the extremes: good luck, misfortune; good hunting, shame; wedding, funeral; good harvest, starvation. "Which way did it go?" the children asked. They should have been in bed long ago. They were so tired, their chores and homework squatting on their evening even on the night of the festival. The teachers for the main belonged to another religion, and the schools did not officially sanction the holiday. Their parents complained that they couldn't depend on the weary children for accurate forecasts. The smoke smarted the children's eyes, while the adults leaned in close and blew the smoke away.

"Not that way! No!" shrieked the children. The parents persisted in bending the fire in the unlucky direction, predicting the children would be eaten by wolves, would fail their math tests, would wet the bed, would fall down stairs, would find their path crossed by a poisonous snail. "No!" the little ones wailed, and the older children joined in, puffing hysterically, warning of hail storms, a cruel assistant principal, a visit from the doctor with his horrid medicine.

These home celebrations were of course a rougher version of what went on in the temples, where the priests chanted strenuously, warding off discomfort and misfortune. The devout gathered on the edges, pledging their own expensive sticks of perfumed wood, and felt virtuous. The fortunes of the wealthy were generally optimistic—deals were predicted to close, new cars would enter the stable, a daughter's wedding was foretold as a glorious celebration.

But the streets around the temples grew darker, as light blazed in the courtyards. Men of the other religion used the occasion to go out in costume. In the old days, they used to spring out at parties going home from temple and chase them, howling. More recently, though, this was a night of rapes and beatings, thrown bricks, familes set upon by masked men with nail-studded clubs.

The fire worshippers responded with arson, or at least they were blamed for the many warehouses that went up crackling, the trash cans lit and rolled down hill, the dry cleaners and fabric shops broken into and torched. The police fought among themselves, and it wasn't necessarily safe to call for help. You couldn't know if they had water or paraffin in their buckets.

Despite that, though, overall, no matter these bad individuals and their violence, wasn't it still a lovely ceremony? Did it matter that these few bad people took advantage? Wasn't it true that the small towns, at least, were still safe? It had long been a tradition to burn empty houses—it was our heritage. People needed their pranks, especially as the cold days set in. All the crime, the fear, the crowded hospital emergency rooms, were outweighed, don't you think, by the wonderful feeling of standing in the garden, a jacket on over pajamas, sweating in front, shivering behind. The ashes circled upwards, swooping like birds, bats, circus tents, one after another. The children couldn't even tell left from right, east from west, and always they swore that the cinder had veered at the last minute over to the lucky direction. And altogether, if you added them all up, most of the cinders went that way, the lucky way. The few turned and swept directly towards tragedy, but mostly, didn't they, for the most part, go the other way?

FIRE II – FILM FESTIVAL

Of course the fire cult celebrated a little differently in Belgrave. The ancient rituals had remained pure, but the worshippers nevertheless embraced new technology. Fifty years ago, they had all flocked to shadow puppet shows for the fire festival, a sheet held in front of a bonfire, human and animal figures shaking fists and paws at each other. Whole extended families of puppeteers raced across the country in their rickety caravans and war-surplus trucks, putting on shows on each of the eight nights of the festival. Thus some towns had a first night showing, others a fourth or seventh, depending on where they sat in the puppeteers' circuit. These numbers had long been associated with each village's name. The young people thought the number was a sort of abandoned postal code, and the older generation periodically berated them for this lapse in knowledge.

In recent times, the film festival had taken over. The capital city monopolized the cinema, though the devout trekked in from the hinterlands, so that shepherds and beet farmers mixed with stars and directors from France, the U.S., India and Australia. For eight nights, the Belgrave Metropole filled every room, even closets and spaces under stairways. The chambermaids shared their quarters with the hairdressers and make-up artists of the actresses. It got so crowded at the Metropole that the young and chic began staying instead at new places they had seen advertised in industry tabloids. These were discount stores forested overnight with partitions to make little bedrooms. The boys serving coffee had never worked the register before, and stared bewildered at the buttons. It took hours to get a greasy, limp croissant. The film buffs huddled in the lobby, still painted the odd pink and teal of the sportswear department it had been three days earlier, and ran their fingers over the ads for restaurants and taverns.

In spite of the trappings of art and glamour, the festival maintained its religious underpinning. Some of the country people had little experience with movies, and they were most fascinated by the light from the projector, especially the way it picked up the dust motes, formerly unseen and now revealed, a whole galaxy hovering above the velvet seats.

Light, fire, was supposed to illuminate and transform. So for some, the stilling of an unruly crowd into a hush of rapt spectators was the mysterious change wrought by the film, regardless of the subject matter. The most religious viewers didn't mind what they saw. They sat composedly, as they had learned in their ashrams, feeling their spirit settle like warm ash around an ember.

Others, though, expected a more strenuous spiritual movement. They wanted to be enlightened and cleansed, burned clean, their vision clarified. This faction of the audience demanded a certain kind of spectacle, scenes that shocked. They wanted prisoners to have guns put to their heads, to see them flinch as sweat stung their eyes, to watch them vomit after the gun misfired and their captor kicked them in the ribs and stomach. If a woman was raped in a basement, they were not content with muffled sounds of sobbing. They needed to know how her attacker had gotten her to open her soft lips over his penis. They demanded an exact brutality.

The directors complied. Though only a minority of the audience were "burners," a special effects industry developed around these tastes. It was the Belgravians who were devout, but hordes of people of no faith across several borders worked with saint-like diligence on movie technology. In their brightly lit workrooms, young men invented plastic patches that looked like a cheek lacerated to the bone. Programmers stayed up all night fiddling with software that digitized dark spaces to make black corners more penetrable. How could a woman's hair look shredded, burned, ripped from the scalp? Specialists around the world mastered the horrific with gels and fans, or with models and lights. Once they had figured out how to make a shadowy garage pulse as a tire iron shattered a skull, it became urgent to use the technology over again so as not to waste it.

The fire festival burned on year round, far from Belgrave, in studios and sound stages, offices and hotel rooms, in decrepit country estates lent for the weekend to a crew who shot a scene in its ancient wine cellar. The hangers-on of the film industry never gave a thought to their eternal souls, or only when they drank themselves sick. Yet without knowing it a kind of salvation clung to them, like a far-away pollen stuck to their fingers.

LITERATURE 1

Trouble with the Southern Empire started gradually. Though they had only recently begun to flaunt their power, they claimed that their culture and civilization was as longstanding and distinguished as Belgrave's. They scoffed at Marmoral. Yet they still scrutinized us.

Marmoral's librarians at first resisted stocking the literature of the Southern Empire, but before long they couldn't avoid it. Imperial publishers sent free examination copies of their scholarly journals, and one-year trial subscriptions. The slim black spines of the imported texts made the Marmolian books look tattered and doughy.

Marmolian academics, of which there were a few, competed with each other for the loveliness of their prose. They wrote their articles and essays out by hand in old, elegant cursive. They gave great thought to punctuation. Marmolian writers employed nine different marks to indicate a pause or stop. One mark indicated that the reader should take a breath, another meant that two closely connected ideas followed each other, enchained. Another meant that the next words would turn the reader's attention away entirely, perhaps to something distracting in the room where he was reading, such as the sweep of his wife's hair as she bent to kiss him. And what if his wife walked by and didn't kiss him, appeared not to notice him frowning in his armchair? In fact, she'd had a lover for three years. Him she sprang to, couldn't wait to press her hands against his chest, she pulled his shirt open and rubbed her head into his neck, wasting some of the few stolen minutes they had together just to inhale him. They only had a half hour to make love, while her daughter was at her piano lesson or while she said she was having her hair cut. Even so, she dawdled over his unbuttoned torso, probing his warm skin. A different mark signaled the end of this interlude, bringing the reader back, settling him again to his task.

The Imperial writers set their words down in lean, muscular strips. They laced abundant quotations from the classics into their sentences with strict, efficient bands. Sometimes one citation after another filled a paragraph, like a judge in a courtroom reading out a charge—count one, murder in the first degree, count two, illegal discharge of a firearm, count three, intent to commit mayhem, count four, unlawful entry, count five—on and on with a sickening, secure confidence.

Some Marmolian academics adopted this style, and occasionally won publication in the Imperial organs. Their colleagues then jeered at them for selling out, but they were secretly jealous. They bought the journal for themselves so they could ponder in private how their fellow had wrenched his words down in that superior, modern way.

The worst was that the Imperial scholars knew more about Marmoral than the Marmolians. Making forays from their hotel rooms, they fastened on minutiae that they set out in Methods and Findings, clearly reproducible steps of their investigations. "Some Marmolian words," they wrote, "change gender. In the countryside, 'bread' is feminine. But the urban gangs use it always in the masculine." They noted down the polite ways women spoke among themselves, and the way mothers called their children. They flattened children's counting and hopscotch songs between the pages of their anthropological journals, draining them of the beating sun the children were supposed to wear hats under, or the cloying rain that kept them indoors all February, fighting with their sisters.

Though some Imperial writers enthused over Marmoral's poetry, they claimed that it was the Marmolians' childlike intensity or naïve trustingness that led to such beautiful images. A man lay down under an almond tree. Forty years earlier, his whole family had been slaughtered in the camps, and all the neighbors from his street. The street itself had been bulldozed, and now other shops sat there, selling the meat forbidden to people of the poet's religion. Did the tree know anything of this? So the Marmoral writers now found their own words clumsy and immature. Each syllable seemed coated with clay, dirt from some native place. If they could have, they would have scrubbed off their fingerprints, used tongs instead of hands, so they could embrace the world like metal on metal. Instead of singing, they would have coughed out neat concrete blocks. They polished and dried the spit off their lips, but their words still retained the regrettable trace of the human.

WORLD ARCHITECTURE

Belgrave, my husband explained to me, had a venerable tradition of science and the humanities. Though the Belgravians were warlike and strong, their generals composed lyric poetry, and even run-of-the-mill radiologists or car dealers had memorized the great chants and lays of the old days in their excellent free public high schools. Belgrave's mathematicians took all the top honors in topology and dominated world geometry conferences. The nation's composers conjured great choral works that sounded like clouds moving through a heavenly rib cage, and its musical theorists took these compositions apart, explaining the chord progressions and the mysticism governing the melodic intervals.

The academic apparatus of the Southern Empire had no choice but to accept Belgrave's scholars as equals, or so my husband claimed. Yet truly, the Belgravians were usually not quite in the first rank. They retained that provincial stamp, seeing everything from a local vantage, the way all their food, from fish to coffee cake, had that taste of saffron. So Belgrave, being a small country, threw all its resources into the few areas where it excelled. Once the southerners had established a million-dollar annual prize for architecture, it seemed possible that a Belgravian could take it.

The architects set up their models in the offices of the world architecture foundation, which spread across the upper floors of what was only for now the tallest building on earth. Looking out over the shoulders of the judges and board members, the Belgravian entrant, the only woman in the room, noted the bundled girders of a half-built structure that would soon overtop this one. Against the orange sun, dozens of construction cranes dipped their iron beaks. The whole city floated in mineral dust as the old neighborhoods were knocked down, wooden houses replaced with brick duplexes, the duplexes razed to make way for six- and seven-story concrete apartment complexes, and these in turn pummeled and carted off so that grand department stores and health clubs could rise up. The photographers had asked her to pose on her hotel balcony the previous evening, at an elegant skirted table swaying in the wind. When she took a sip from her wine glass, a gray scum of concrete particles transferred to her lip. She could still feel the grit on her teeth.

Out of the hundreds of entrants, only the five finalists were left to present their work. All except the woman from Belgrave were Imperial citizens with museums and luxury shopping centers to their credit, who had designed skyscrapers and city ports, corporate headquarters, concert halls. The judges asked the architects to explain their models. The first to go showed his recreation center, made of folded glass with seams reinforced with diamond dust. Seen from a distance, the whole thing blazed silver. From close up, however, it shimmered like water. From the eastern and western sides, it appeared like an undulating glass wave, but from head on, it revealed itself an abstracted dolphin with an arched, leaping back. "Joy," said its designer, "creativity, sparkle, play."

Another entrant had modeled a series of pyramids, like those in Egypt, but no bigger than shoe boxes. However, these opened out underground into vast terraces filled with warm, wood-paneled offices, the headquarters of the Southern Empire's leading insurance company. The next entrant showed a complex of elegant villas. He had taken the ancient wood joinery technique of the area's indigenous carpenters and married it to slabs of raw, rusted steel. The hilltop complex combined the folk charm of a shanty town with the craftsmanship of a royal doll's house.

The next was a private dwelling designed for an old couple who both suffered from Alzheimer's. Its architect had sewn thousands of frog skins together, inflated them into a balloon, and anchored the sphere in a glacial lake surrounded by a dense pine forest. He lined the interior walls with moss, and the old couple crept along the spiral hallways, lost in a soft green murk. An elevator constantly floated from floor to floor. If the old people grew afraid or confused, soon enough they would find themselves back again in the central vestibule, where the elevator lifted them either up or down. The house bobbed in the silent water, always a soothing, subtle motion.

It seemed nothing could be better than any of these. The Imperial architects arrived at work early in the morning and stayed until after sundown, eating noodles and sandwiches delivered to their desks, while they sketched and computed and talked to clients on the phone. They lashed each other on to more and more spectacular buildings, fed by the enormous fortunes of the empire's burgeoning industries. In half an hour, the architects might design three car parks, a resort and a sock factory, they were so fast and skilled and efficient. It was ridiculous to think a woman from stodgy Belgrave could compete with these roaring modernists.

The Belgravian's building was nothing but a ball of tar. It had no interior space, but was densely, darkly material. The judges had seen it already, but the other architects had only heard vague rumors. They pressed in closer. "What is it for?" they asked her.

"It calms your thoughts," she said. "Once you think something in here, it can't escape again. Lunatics who obsess over aliens in ceiling fans are finally relieved of their fears. If you wonder if you are not quite living up to what your mother meant for you to be, this worry disappears. The sight of your ex-lover's hairbrush, which she never claimed from your bedroom, stops tormenting you." But how do you get in, they all wondered? How do you get out again?

"It's somewhat final," she said simply. There was no air in it, no door, no window. Nothing but tar.

They shook their heads. How had she ever been allowed to enter the contest? The prize went, not too surprisingly, to the wood and steel villas. These represented all that was foremost about the empire, its march forward, retaining the beauty and dignity of the past, but making all new. Journalists surged around the winner. They knew him well. He had been runner-up the year before. He gave a speech that was witty and touching, then his compatriots splashed him with champagne. The woman flew back to Belgrave the next day, and on Monday was back at her drafting table. She assumed she had been forgotten. She hadn't made friends with the other contestants, they had not invited her onto their listservs or told her they hoped to run into her at future meetings. Yet her Imperial colleagues did think of her sometimes, pausing with their arms reaching for a new pencil, then setting their hands back on their laps. Was it possible they had made some kind of mistake, forgotten something? Was there a door at the end of the office hallway that was locked, and always stayed locked? Had they left the kettle on at home, and the house burned down?

Was it worth it to get up in the morning, to shave and eat, to put on a clean shirt? Surely these thoughts had plagued them before, but they came into sharper focus, became more insistent. The architects met in the bar down the street at the end of the day and ordered a whisky, and another one, before catching the train.

TOURISM

The Belgravians traveled frequently to Marmoral to observe our charming folk customs. Honeymooners booked a week at our island pleasure palace in the town of Let, and university students signed on for a river cruise, to gamble and drink their April break away. Journalists hoping to revive a stale career begged their editors to send them to Marmoral. Even the simplest description of a waitress whipping cream in a farmhouse restaurant won over readers at home. How quaint, how foolish, our sisters and brothers across the border. By knowing them, we come to know ourselves.

And hadn't everyone heard the legend of the Marmoral wolf-men? The little villages in the pine forests locked themselves up tight at night. The women's first duty in the morning was to sweep the yard free of animal tracks, because if the dew filled a werewolf's paw print, and by some accident the liquid touched innocent skin, a new werewolf was created.

"Then couldn't there be wolf-women, too?" queried the journalist Franz. Twenty years ago he had made his name covering the trial of an infamous poisoner, but he hadn't done much he was proud of recently. He had renewed his passport, updated his inoculations, and trekked to the remotest hinterlands of Marmoral. He could barely understand the woman's thick Marmoral accent, though he enjoyed her low pitch, the way the words slunk over the fullness of her lips.

"The women," she said, "can't stand the force of the transformation."

"Then how could a little boy of four?"

Instead of answering, she stared at him, and he sank his eyes to his coffee. The bed at the inn was too hard, and his shoulders and back ached. It had taken him three weeks to track down this woman. She made her living as a potter, turning out the matte black bowls the area was known for. Marmoral ware had had a vogue in Belgrave a few years ago. Its stark simplicity mixed well with crystal and silver, not that Franz had paid much attention. But he would bring a few pieces back for his girlfriend and his sister.

The journalist bummed around for another couple days. He mailed in a few stories and sketched some more in his notebook. None of it was really right, though, and he made his way back to the potter's house. Everyone said she looked after her werewolf brother, it was no secret at all. He begged her to let him watch, hidden safely in a tree.

"I don't know what you're talking about," she said. But he persuaded her to let him treat her to dinner at the inn in the guise of an interview with a well-known artisan. She met him in a dress from his mother's era, a fluffy lilac and lace thing that hung on her charmlessly. Black grime still lined her fingernails, but she had skewered her thick hair back into a shapely bun. His friends would have laughed at him, shoveling in the plain Marmoral bean soup under the greasy gas light.

He walked her back to her cottage, his boots clunking against the hard dirt path. Her little leather slippers made no noise at all. The moon sifted its white light down on them through the slits between the branches. Her neighbors had shut all their shutters tight, letting out no chinks of yellow. Crickets chirred all around, but no human voices chatted or mumbled from the porches and yards.

She invited him in and poured him a glass of liqueur. He was amused at her tiny faceted goblets, when the strong, pine-scented drink would have seemed more natural in one of her black clay tumblers. Already he was putting the night into prose for his readers in Belgrave, highlighting the remoteness of the village, detailing the streaks of clay that seemed permanently worn into her forearms. "So I said good night," he wrote, "and off I went, back along the haunted track."

Now he was telling the story to his girlfriend and their friends Sara and Paul, sitting around the coffee table in his girlfriend's apartment. "I'd been on that path not twenty minutes earlier, and there wasn't a wrong turn to take on it, but suddenly it ended right in front of an enormous tree."

"You must have been pretty drunk," said Paul, and they all glugged more wine into their glasses. He pulled his girlfriend onto his lap, but she squirmed away, laughing. "And out from behind the tree comes this huge wolf," he went on, "staring right at me with green glowing eyes. It's moaning, growling, but somehow I understand its speech: 'What have you done to my sister?'"

His girlfriend, creasing her forehead, wound her hand around his bicep, making him slop his wine.

"Weren't you scared?"

"I was terrified, terrified," he said, mopping at his lap with a napkin. His hand struck him as unnaturally black. Dense fur gleamed up at him. He dropped the napkin as yellow claws thrust out of his fingertips.

"So what did you do?" whispered his girlfriend. His eyes fixed on the plump flesh of her neck, flushed and pulsing. He lunged at her, pinning her under him. He ripped into her shoulder. Her blood spurted against his teeth, a marvelous warm smack, and he burrowed his snout into the wound. He felt everything in its different textures, her tendons slithering apart, her bones splintering up into his gums. His friends' hands dug into him, pulling him back, but he went on, dragging his claws through the buttery skin of her belly. If only he could have stopped narrating it, the nouns and verbs even now beading through his skull in their endless chains. Only a little more, as a chair leg bashed him across the spine and his teeth snapped through her spongy breast. Just a little longer, and he would stop observing, making notes, composing. A howl wrenched out of his throat, though even as he heard the sound, he thought, 'A howl wrenched out of my throat.'

"A little more?" asked the potter, tipping the decanter over his glass. His girlfriend's head lolled sideways, blood streaming through her hair.

"A little more," he croaked. "Fill it. Fill it."

ARACHNE

My husband discovered a new brothel in the back streets behind Belgrave's capital. I didn't need to know about it, did I? But he couldn't help it, he said. It wasn't like he'd gone looking for it. It was part of the culture. The brothel had no name, not even a sign over the door. For all his protest that the people of Belgrave were altogether more noble and civilized than my Marmolians, his country had no towns of any size other than its ungainly, sprawling capital. In a former sandwich shop a block to the west of the parliament building, an old woman had moved in with a new crew of girls. Just down the street were two of Belgrave's oldest houses of prostitution, centuries-old hereditary businesses that were in all the guidebooks. These featured red lights, pink curtains, filmy nightgowns, seventeen-year-old beauties from the mountain villages. The girls shopped together in the markets in the late afternoon, where people goggled at their thin foreign tee shirts and stove pipe jeans, their modern, confident allure.

I don't suppose I was too happy about Belgrave's flourishing sex industry, but this new place was made along different lines. When it rained, its dim doorway was barely visible. Even a man's very first approach to it was a hesitant groping, a brushing of fingertips along contrasting textures—rusty chain link, splintered wood, the smooth, sticky plastic of a shower curtain that partially shielded the porch. Madame specialized in exotics—not the brash magazine-reading girls of the other institutions, but women widened, enhanced, enlarged, or made tighter. One was slashed to accommodate "you and your friend," while a host were permanent virgins, sewed enticingly tight. Another was totally hairless, even her eyebrows and arm hair removed for all-over silkiness, while another had velvety, furry breasts. One had been fitted with gripping, stippled vaginal walls. I would have preferred vague wondrous claims— unforgettable! Like nothing you've ever experienced! But the exercise of inventing Belgrave had made my husband, like me, into a wielder of precise optical detail.

We had little to do with each other in the evenings now. "What's new?" he sometimes asked, standing four feet behind me in the kitchen, watching me turn down the flame under a pot of rice and punch the timer. He was afraid to ask when dinner would be ready. Maybe I hadn't made enough for two. He didn't like my cooking any more, anyway. I ate plain rice, a handful of cashews, an apple. That was enough. Or I cooked an elaborate eggplant dish, a curry braised in coconut milk, and by the time it was done, Daniel had already had some bread, a piece of ham, some carrots, three cookies. Our meal times were all out of synch, and our going to bed and rising.

One evening he told me a new attraction had arrived at the brothel. "Was there an ad?" I asked Daniel.

Just a rumor, word of mouth. "You won't like it, though."

Yes, the whole thing disgusted me. I had used to love his hair, especially when it flopped over his eyes when he neglected to get it cut. These days he was keeping it combed and parted, in yet another affront to me. His walk was more firm, too. I had used to light up to his heavy, rapid tread on the stairs, back in our old place. His decisiveness, which traveled through his every gesture, had in those days been reassuring. "No one will say what it is," he said. "Just something different."

"A thing or a she?" I asked. Without answering, he walked into the living room to turn on the lamps.

He wouldn't tell me any more. I fretted as the gray behind the curtains became black. If I had to imagine it myself, it would be far worse than if he just told me. But he only rummaged on his shelf of miscellaneous things, looking for a washer to fit the leaky bathroom sink.

Men had to pay up front to be led into the back room where Madame kept her special wonders. A man who ran a chain of pet shops hurried out of the room shaking his head, his hands thrust into his pants pockets as if to keep them from touching anything else. A couple of mobster louts leaned against the wall for a bit, deciding whether to go upstairs again, or maybe to go out to Kipp's Bar. Madame smiled at them, and they fled. Nothing was worse than the sight of her even teeth making a friendly gesture in a face so closed off. Now the room was empty, and she sat down on the sofa and turned on the television.

Arachne wondered at the sound of the tv. It chattered on, girls talking, a horse neighing, the swift approach of booted feet. Then a long pause, a soft "oh," a swell of saxophone. She lounged against the pillows, her swollen abdomen mounded in front of her. The body of a spider, the torso of a woman, slender neck rising above heavenly breasts, and such a sad, sweet face, while down below, her strange bulbous mid-section could not be confined by the crumpled sheets. She sighed and clacked her little hindlegs. She could not move off the bed without help, and Madame had hired two men to roll her. They were supposed to swab out the gummy orifice where she made her silk—it was in their job description—but they refused. Madame had to do this herself, with a dowel wrapped in wool, like the dusters maids used to get cobwebs off the ceiling.

What had she been like when she was a normal girl? A weaver, from a long line of weavers, the gifted youngest sister in a family renowned for its rugs and tapestries. Her sisters and aunts petted and praised her, spoiled her. "No one can equal my skill," she said, when she was just fourteen years old. The goddess of weaving came down from the clouds to investigate this claim. In the guise of an old woman, she knocked on Arachne's door.

"No," said Daniel, leaning over me, the ends of a roll of plumber's tape in his hand. "That's not it at all."

Arachne at seventeen was the village beauty, the butcher's only child. She stood behind the counter, chops at her fingertips, sausages swinging overhead. Her fingers were always red with blood, her apron smeared, her lips a scarlet gash. When she was tired, she waved her hair off her forehead with the back of her hand, and her bangs too stiffened with blood. The little membranes that sealed off kidneys and livers came loose and clung to her sleeves. When she came out in the sun at the end of the day, she picked these off, and the blobs of fat and marrow from her skirt. The young men were afraid of her chiseled features, her short, sharp laugh delivered while looking elsewhere. They only approached her quietly, secretly, after having walked their other girlfriend home and said good night. She had one man, then another, then another. They all knew each other, yet didn't know they had all been entangled with her. How sad they were in the evenings now, even when newly married, the wife expecting their first child. Something about Arachne, how she held them close, cooing into their hair, but then later she wouldn't even glance up. It penetrated and left them dry, no good for anything else. They poked at the fire, but never felt any warmer. The sun barely shone now, but only looked down on them, scornful.

"No, I don't think so at all," I said. But Daniel went on.

I still thought the goddess had come knocking, had challenged Arachne to a contest. Arachne wove the most marvelous scarf, on which was portrayed the entire history of her village—its founding by two bear cubs, the great fire, the flood, the invasion of the barbarians in great-grandfather's time, the clever girl who outwitted the army with her poppy seeds, the modern-day back streets where the tanner caste slept in the doorways of the spinners' hovels, and the weavers, three streets over, who watered the geraniums in pots on their balconies. She wove pigeons cleaning their breast feathers, and antelope, field mice, wood lice. Even the peace of a moonlit evening, when the girls and their aunts played cards on the veranda, was captured in the floating strands of Arachne's scarf.

Yet the goddess got out her loom and proceeded to lay down with her shuttle the very cracking of the cosmos as it exploded from its seed, and emptiness, deserts, doubt, the shade of anxiety you feel when you turn a corner and the street is empty, though well-lit. A friend tells you a story about his uncle who moved to a derelict farm in his twenties and stayed there tending raspberries and rutabagas for forty years, working every day alone in silence for ten to twenty hours, and you feel so helpless, always distracted, doing nothing worthwhile. This was in the goddess's tapestry, as well as watching your father stumble against the coffee table in the throes of the stroke that killed him, and the enormity of a mistake you made years earlier when you married someone you weren't sure you loved. All was delineated in soft silk, the abstract weight of the universe overshadowing the historical and particular.

"This is what she was," said Daniel. "A cruel, withholding girl. Always she whispered that she loved her man, but each one was only the latest conquest. She didn't care at all. She had no pity, no feeling. Only an immense pleasure in her own attractiveness. Until one of her lovers cursed her, and made her a spider. 'I see what you're doing,' he said, 'drawing me in.' This one man wouldn't stand for her soft looks that were only binding him up."

"Wait," I said. But Daniel had already described the way Arachne's slender waist all the sudden sucked in. It became no bigger than her wrist, while her rear grew globular, heavy, spherical. Her legs withered into tiny clicking sticks. Her hair fell in piles on the floor around her. She looked in wild anxiety at her mirror, at her dressing table with its bottles of lotion and perfume. The summer dress she wore under her butcher's smock would never fit her again, but hung on its nail, now ready for some other girl. She would have to flee the village before light so no one would see her in her terrible new manifestation.

"But her face?" I said. I had seen her looking so remorseful, tears shining in the corners of her eyes.

"Oh, well," he said. "We have to leave her a little bit of the human, don't we?"

"Yes," I said. I ran to the bedroom to look in the mirror.

STOP

"Stop," I said. "Let's not do this anymore."

For weeks we had done nothing but manufacture these stories for each other. Summer had eased into September. I had put blankets back on the bed and started to worry again about the winter heating bills. We were coming up on the date Daniel had circled on the calendar, when he would take his boots in for resoling. We should have been thinking about bugging the landlord again to fix the broken storm door he had failed to have repaired a year ago. Of course we'd have to agree on whose responsibility it was to do some of the little jobs before us—buying double-sided tape and plasticing up the windows, plugging the holes where the mice would rush in the first night it got cold. Daniel probably had a long list of things that needed doing, that I should have been doing half of, but I couldn't count on him to tell me what these were.

"What if we got a dog?" I said. "We could walk her in the evenings, rambling around the neighborhood, looking in people's windows when they haven't drawn the curtains yet."

I was unable to conceive because of some earlier complications, and we had stopped discussing that.

"Is that how you see us now," he said, "out for an evening stroll with Sheppie?"

"Sheppie!" I said. "Or Biscuit."

That's all we needed to do, walk down the street, our gloved hands sometimes bumping. That would have been enough for me. When we first met, he'd told me a particularly vivid dream he'd had about me, that he had been standing in line at the grocery store and I was at the next station. I had come over to his line, to stand behind him, and neither of us had spoken. He was strongly affected by this dream, the simple offering of my company. He used to plead with me not to leave him. 'Even if I ask you to go,' he said, 'I need you to remember that you shouldn't.' I had promised to stay with him no matter what, but privately I didn't consider this kind of contract enforceable.

FIRE III – FIREFLIES

So we stopped for a little while, as the evenings got cooler and the sirens on Central, half a mile distant, cut more sharply. We went out to dinner once, but both felt bad about the money. We were both working but, as you know, things were getting more and more expensive.

"What about fireflies?" I said.

"What about them?"

"The ones in Marmoral are different."

"Oh," he said. "I thought they might be."

I couldn't tell if he wanted to hear the rest. I was darning socks, both his and mine. I didn't really know how to do it, but I thought it might be better than having to buy new ones. I would have liked to close the holes up neatly, drawing the frayed edges down to a tight dark spot. But my awkward stitches turned the holes into rigid half moons, as if the socks were now scarred from their adventures, aching, limping.

Half of Marmoral's people celebrated fire. The priests of the fire cult bred a species of firefly that was larger but more delicate than the wild ones. These pampered creatures passed their larval stages under logs which the priests gently sprinkled with water or dried with fans, as the weather dictated. For three days only they lived in their adult incarnation, dull tan beetles with blinking yellow abdomens. For the short period the fireflies came out, the members of the fire cult stayed up all night, evading official curfew, and walked around the orchards. The dark trees flashed, leaves suddenly visible, then shrank back to murky umbrellas as the bugs' torsos shut down. Your lover's face swung into focus, the phosphorescence behind her haloing her cheek. Then a moment later she was extinguished, just a black figure beside you. Yet you still heard her breathing, regular and steady.

The fireflies didn't do well after the introduction of modern pesticides. By the seventies they were almost all gone. They were enshrined in a song the children had to learn in Sunday school. While the little ones, under the spell of their beautiful teacher, chanted the lines with pious awe, by the time they were nine or ten they were sick to death of the nostalgic religion lessons and fitted their own words to the hymn's simple rhyme. "Her tits, her tits," they sang as loudly as they could. But if their mother suddenly showed up, they went back to the original version.

Recently, with only a day's warning, the city administrators in the capital sent work crews to tear up the main street through the shopping district of the fire worshippers. The waste pipes underneath needed to be replaced. Everyone had complained for years about the sewers backing up, but they were still affronted by the quick work of the bulldozers. And when the workers showed up at dawn, cut through concrete for an hour, and then vanished to smoke cigarettes and watch soccer at the cafes in adjoining streets, the sour views of those who saw the construction project as punitive seemed justified. The workers set up sawhorses across every intersection. It became almost impossible to travel from one side of the district to the other, and the roads leading out were capriciously closed, one on one day, another the next, so that you never knew if all your maneuvering to reach a certain street was any good at all. The workmen came back in late afternoon and hammered through the dinner hour. All their effort seemed to do nothing but stir up dust. They knocked out electricity and phone lines and took days to restore service. Women stumbled to their dress shops, their fashionable shoes no good on the jagged rubble. The upholsterer didn't get his delivery because the supply truck couldn't make it through. Finally he sent his son and a lot of little boys to meet the truck in a park a mile away. The kids filed back to the shop, carrying the bolts of velvet like corpses between them.

It was unbearable, an outrage, and after months of work, the street seemed no nearer completion than on the first day. It would have been okay to have the sewers still back up, the residents told each other. At least they had their own plumbers. Wasn't the city tormenting them? And who knows if there wouldn't be a special tax levied, to make them pay for it all. That would be no surprise.

But each evening around nine o'clock, the workmen melted away. With no traffic on it, the main street was remarkably quiet. The kids from the apartment houses came out to play in the dirt. It was like when they visited their cousins back home in the countryside. Their parents came out to call them in, but the kids paid no attention. And the parents didn't really mind. They stood on the corners talking to their neighbors, some they knew, some strangers from other floors or other buildings. The workmen left flashing orange flares on the sawhorses. All along the torn-up street, the harsh lights switched on and off, regular but out of synch with each other. Little slices of storefront stepped on stage, then fell back into shadow, one after another down the strip. If the electricity came back on, people hurried home to watch the news. But on the nights when the lines remained disconnected, men and women dragged out chairs or stretched out blankets and stayed up til all hours. The orange flares lit up rings of desolate rock, overturned chunks of concrete and orphaned pipe joins. The street might never be fixed. Rumor had it the city would leave it unfinished until the residents forked over a special assessment. The landlords should have paid it, but it was to be exacted from the tenants, and until everyone had settled their bill, the street would remain a mess. The workers were to dig holes one day and fill them the next. The cost would go up and up. It was intolerable, unfair, a disaster.

The children heard all this but didn't let on. They crept down into the craters and tunnels under the street. They didn't care how dangerous it was. Even if their father shook them and made them promise, they still crawled under. "Her tits, her tits," they sang from their hiding places. The adults sang back, somewhat ashamed of how sentimental the real words were. What a stupid song. Everyone knew the melody, and some just hummed that. All up and down the street it burst out, little pockets of sound.

WORDS 1

"Well then, let me tell you this," he said.

Throughout its long history, Belgrave had withstood many attacking barbarians, and had in turn expanded its borders by taking over the measly city-states of upstart pirates and robber barons. It was a wonder Marmoral hadn't been totally absorbed.

The frequent invasions, mergers, and acquisitions left the populace struggling for a common language. The Belgravians for the main stuck to their own tongue, which was well suited for argument, contracts, litigation, inventories, and hero tales. But the common people ended all their sentences with "eh?" If they didn't speak other languages entirely, they slipped in adopted words. These foreign expressions, like terms for "afternoon nap," "redouble an insult," or for specific tasks of imported industries like synthetic hormone manufacturing, had no Belgravian equivalent. So they had their uses. But these imports struck the upright Belgravians like cat hair in a salad—women should tie their hair back before entering the kitchen, and should brush their clothes, too, if they are going to spend hours reading in a chair with the cat in their lap. And then, when a black thunderstorm passes in late afternoon so that the sky plunges into darkness and after half an hour clears up, and the evening is then lighter than five o'clock so that time seems to be going backwards, well, we don't have to have a word for that. We could simply stand on the porch and look out, no one saying anything. That is really best.

In any case, many educated Belgravians were careful to strain their speech of foreign terms, passing all their utterances through a sieve before speaking. Their great-grandfathers, they maintained, the classic statesmen who had built the courthouse, cathedral, and capitol dome, had carefully packed their meaning into each word, sending them out one by one like little boats or cheese pastries. A conversation with such a speaker was like a continual birthday, each party eagerly unwrapping and examining their gifts. Thus when husband and wife got into an argument, and she said, "But that's what you *said!*" he could then find his words on the floor, the meaning lying around casually between their feet, and show her, see, *this* is what I said!

But if she wasn't convinced, she might go on looking, and eventually pick up the wrong words, or older ones that had blown around the room for a time, maybe even years. For this reason the foreign women didn't make good maids. They had too much to think about. The corners of rooms got all cluttered up with their own mutterings—*where is my husband, I don't believe he was with his brother last night, I can't feed three children on my own, I should have hanged myself that night when I was so drunk at Mama's party last year, but I mustn't, I mustn't.*

And no matter what the teachers wrote on the blackboard in the parochial schools, the children found their words not clean and concise, but attached to long, sticky strings. You should be more careful, said their mothers, as if her own utterances were always cheerful gateaus, chocolates criss-crossed with icing. The daughter, fifteen, spat her vocabulary out in front of the mirror in her room with the door shut. No matter what she did, her words were burdened with flanges, long limp tails. She examined them one at a time and judged them, misshapen, so ugly, just boring, so wrong. She vowed that one day she would learn to say exactly what she meant.

Belgrave's bad-boy philosopher came up with something new. He expelled each word half-formed—unskinned, incredibly light utterances that floated delicately away from him and only gained their shells when they came in contact with someone else's speech. He created a mongrel poetry, a racket sport, and a cure for melancholy, which were all in fact the same tool. His mistress stood behind him and massaged his shoulders when he had been working half the night. But he knew she had another lover, his former student. She stayed with him whenever he, the philosopher, had an engagement out of town. She forwarded her phone so he couldn't tell she wasn't home. He could almost ignore it, but not quite.

When they went to parties, all of Belgrave swirled around them. One after another journalists and politicians took him into a corner to ask him to clarify some points in his latest essay. "You're looking well," said the Minister of Education. "Never better," he said, and the minister laughed as if this was the wittiest thing yet.

WORDS II

Given that Marmoral was governed by thieves, the people developed a unique way of speaking. "Fresh meat" meant essentially nothing, as the butcher called everything he sold "fresh," regardless of age, plumping the roasts with injections of water, dying the chops pink, bleaching the gray hamburger. The jewelers sold both emeralds and their green glass twins at either astronomical prices or dirt cheap. It all depended on whether the customer wanted to flaunt his wealth by spending big or to get away with a bargain. The jewelers didn't even know how to tell real stones from fake, or said they didn't. It wasn't a useful skill. Value and price were entirely situational.

Marmoral's words were shifty, slightly billowing bags, shimmering with the light of whatever was said around them. A mother called her daughter—"I haven't heard from you in a year. I know you're busy, but I worry." The daughter answered, "Everything is fine. It's just the children are underfoot all the time." This meant she was tired to death, and resented her mother's words before she got married. She knew he was a gambler, but he was good-hearted, really he was. She often thought of coming home, piling the kids on the train. But she wouldn't do it. She would never go back.

Do you think her mother understood all that? Yes, perfectly.

Marmoral developed its written language from Belgrave's, taking the neat Belgravian letters and stretching them, folding them, making them more flowing. Written notes were as good for thieving as anything else. "I have tried to reach you several times by phone, but you were never in," began a letter to a creditor. "Payment will follow soon. Let me explain the circumstances exactly."

In the last century, Marmoral's head librarian decided to write a dictionary. He drove around the provinces in a donkey cart, collecting words. He began with names of birds, then types of cloth and other household goods, curse words, children's names. The villagers locked their doors against him. When he caught one old woman out sweeping her yard, she wasn't much help. "That's a cardinal," she said. "That's a chicken." She told him the woodland birds had no names. They were just birds. She demanded payment for her contribution. But he knew the names of thrushes and woodpeckers himself. He had grown up around here. The ones he didn't remember he made up. His dictionary, when completed, was spectacularly inaccurate.

Even so, the university students foamed about it. It was a wicked thing, pinning our words down, when all our heritage was looseness, vagueness. The members of their little political group organized to break into the library at night and let the words out of the book. It was very hard to scrape them up. The librarian had stuck them down with hide glue, and the more resistant ones he nailed as well. Often they injured the words as they liberated them. "Scrub brush," from the household word category, meant also hard work, hard assed, diligent, and of course also lazy, butt ugly, a frigid woman or a stupid man. In a poem it might mean also the simple, deadening tasks of home, that one however longed for when cooped up in the town. There might be a kind of integrity to "scrub brush," and of course it had great proximity to a mother's hands. If a man hesitated to marry his sweetheart because he imagined her years from now, stooped over the washing, and he would rather keep things as they were, her pretended diffidence in front of her family, her wild clinging to him in the orchard late at night, all that might be expressed in scrub brush, or even door stop, dish soap. It was these more complex definitions that got cut off when the students tore the words free. Sometimes only the literal meaning survived. The word hunched into itself, drawn in with pain, and when nursed to health it was okay, but never the same.

The librarian got the government to hire armed guards. They policed the reading room and stacks during the day and paced the perimeter of the building by night. The guards' footsteps echoed around the silent square while the students lay on their bellies, timing the rounds with stop watches. They pulled off one last raid and tore sheets and sheets out of the dictionary after cutting through the barbed wire that penned it in. All those words died, so suddenly yanked into freedom that they went into shock. The hasty students chiseled them off the paper and set them on branches or wrapped them in blankets. They were revolutionaries, without much sense of husbandry. They argued about proper care while the freed words shriveled with cold, or crept off by themselves to lodge in cracks between the floorboards.

As a result, Marmolians, those great lovers, had to express their feelings in the stock phrases of Hallmark cards. "Do you love me?" "Yes," they said, when before they would have conveyed the same thing by referring to oak trees, sand bars, even the sound of a woman clipping her nails in the evening. The crickets made their racket unimpeded in the garden, while inside, he listened to the similar quiet click click as she busied herself in the bathroom before coming to bed. What state was he in that he quivered to hear that sound, and how familiar it had grown, though they'd only known each other a month now.

But all that, as I said, was a hundred years ago. Since that time, the people of Marmoral had to content themselves with a simpler, more practical vocabulary.

TELENOVELAS

Despite the diminution of their language, and doesn't that happen everywhere, all the time, the Marmolians were known for their storytelling. In the old days, the puppet shows ran on endlessly, the audience sometimes arguing with the characters—"Go back to her, you idiot! She really loves you!"

Now the towns shut down at one o'clock, and even herders and farm hands spent whole paychecks on tiny tvs so they could tune into the daily serial. For six years, Scott and Rachel argued. They were clearly no good for each other. She had a child by his brother while he slept with the nurse, the candy store girl, the evil Claudia, and even an older woman, a friend of his mother's. But when at last they moved into separate houses and became no more than friends, the light seemed to dim all over Marmoral. Sure it was better for both of them, and the children too. They had at last matured and done the responsible thing. No need to make each other miserable.

Half the country wrote them letters commending their decision. But at the same time, ratings sank. The teachers who had told the children to "read quietly" while they stole off to the teacher's lounge now stayed in the classroom all afternoon. They told themselves it was because the principal might drop by. But he had turned off his tv too, and spent the one o'clock hour aimlessly tapping his pencil over his charts of salaries and expenses.

Fortunately, it all started up again when Clarisse ran off one night after slashing Brad with a kitchen knife. He slapped her when he was drunk, but she wouldn't stand for him twisting her arm. With the few dollars in her purse, she paid the bus driver to drop her in the next town. There she became a sales representative for a textbook firm and traveled by company car to colleges and bookstores. She drank with the buyers after hours in paneled lounges until she hooked up with a man even better-looking than Brad, though obviously a troubled sort.

Clarisse's boyfriend was hard to locate by day, secretive and suave, with an old mother he was constantly going off to visit. Meanwhile, Clarisse became weaker, her vision blurry by noon. Her new friends noticed the change, though she did not—her pale skin, her red lips. "It's Steve," they said. "Didn't you know? His first wife died, his second went insane. He is in fact a vampire."

She took him to court, embittered over money he had borrowed to invest in a strip mall medical lab. She rose white and shaking in front of the judge. Steve had not shown up. "What I want to know," she said, "is why he forgot my birthday. It was just yesterday, and he says he loves me."

What kind of love is it when he's sucking your blood? Give up, said her viewers. Clarisse, save yourself.

No, she said. I've never felt like this about anyone. If he's really a vampire, why aren't I dead? If you only knew what it's like when we're alone together. The camera had never shown them sleeping curled up, her head against his chin. Sometimes he woke her with his snoring and she gently turned him over, saying "Sweetie? Sweetie?" No one had witnessed her look down her body when they were making love, the cave between their chests funneling down to their black joined groins.

He stole your money. He keeps earth from his grave in his desk drawer.

That's not what matters, she said. (Though if that was true, why was she in court?) She thought of the first time she'd seen him, laughing in the corner booth with some other girl. As soon as he looked over at her, he stopped smiling, grew serious. He was so pleasant and relaxed with everyone else. But it had taken him months to even say hello to her.

LITERATURE 11

If Belgrave had a master novel, the one everyone read and referred to, saw themselves as characters in, it would begin with a man standing in the alley burning trash in a can. The sun sets behind the row houses. Light filters red through the leaves of the junky trees. The bend in his neck means he's thinking, but of what? Still the countess? Seven years he was away fighting the civil war. In the dazzle of flares and tracer bullets, she walked towards him. Extending his hand to touch her cheek, he fell into a collapsed tunnel. The tanks trundled over his head, their treads flinging the arms and legs of his companions left and right. Their brains rained down on him, filthed his hair. But she was near, if he could only find her.

He could not have known that despite her promises, she had married a banker, a mathematician, who was useful to both warring sides. But even he tripped up, and soldiers locked them in a gravekeeper's hut. She picked the mouse turds off the bread that was thrown them. She knew somewhere a mill still ground wheat, and boys brought firewood to a bakery. Though she had never loved her husband, he was kind, like furniture. Years later she remained grateful for chairs that heaved their softness under her so she didn't have to touch the cold, wet earth.

How many times had she saved him, the trash burner, arriving at an abandoned farmhouse as dark fell to say, "Run into the woods now, it's not safe." He followed her lantern through the swamp; she beckoned him back into the doorway just as the general rode by. The soldiers of the other side torched a shed where prisoners hid. Flames shot up and out, creating a new outline, the spare wooden rectangle transforming into her shoulders draped in a ball dress.

When the high school students wrote their essays, they knew not to offend the teacher. They had taken dutiful notes on his lectures on the symbolism of the chandelier. They reproduced his themes in their assignments, not daring to say how tedious it was. Some kept their distance from the book, made sure it had nothing to do with them. In fact they read only the abridged version, an outline with chapter summaries, or read the first fifty pages, then harangued their one diligent friend—tell us what happens in the end. In the movie she passed him in the street, not noticing him. He only recognized her because of the ring she still wore. He was mute; she was blind. This was not interesting to seventeen-year-olds, who chattered all day long and zinged their eyes over cars, tv, tee shirts, magazines. "This great work has stamped our national character," they wrote, having changed the words around a bit from the samples in the cheat books. The teacher graded their essays on a scale of one to five. The countess caressed the silk fringes of her pillows. How good the world was, to go on and on. The trash burner knocked on the back gate. The cook didn't hear him over her own cheerful singing.

WAIT

That man came into the copy room again when I couldn't get away. I didn't know if it was just accidental or whether he saw me go by and followed me in. I had only had a year of community college before my first disastrous half a pregnancy knocked me out for a bit. By the time I was ready to go back, the city had shut down its loan program. I had gotten in during the last good year, a final spurt of government generosity before everything dried up. I was lucky to hang onto my filing job, my office dogsbody job. I wasn't qualified for much else. The hot, rhythmic roar of the copier wasn't so bad, the light roaming back and forth under the lid, a caged panther keeping its eye on me.

"Oh, you're here," he said. I couldn't think how to answer that. I turned my back to him and picked the paper clips off the next sets of documents. This would get them all mixed up if I wasn't careful.

He had to call his broker, he said. Though no one was making money in this market, he was at least holding steady or only going down by one or two percent. "It's hard," he said. "Three years ago I had so much money I didn't know what to do with it. I bought the stupidest car."

I had to lift the cover and do the next things one by one on the glass. He leaned against the table and fingered the sets of papers I'd already finished.

"Look at how neat you got these all stapled," he said. I had actually taken the trouble to get the metal lined up at the same precise angle. I looked up at him to see if he was making fun of me. He didn't seem to be. His face was red, though maybe it always mostly was. He surely had better things to be doing. He could have sent Susanna to do his copying.

The copy room was nothing more than a closet, no windows, the air heated from the machine and perfumed with ink. I wouldn't be able to get to the door without squeezing past his hips.

"I have a lot to do," I said. "You should come back in twenty minutes."

"Okay," he said. "What time is it?"

He picked up my wrist with his thumb and forefinger and brought my watch up to his face. It was a light grip, just on the leather band. I stood absolutely still. He didn't look at me, just at my hand, which had no wedding ring, as to me and Daniel such a symbol hadn't seemed important. He didn't twist me towards him. It seemed only his fingers and my wrist existed in the room and we were two zoologists watching their interaction from behind glass. He had told me before about his stock portfolio, and said I had an interesting face. "Are you Greek?" he asked me. "Are you Catholic?" I didn't joke about him with Julie and Susanna. I didn't go by his desk if I could help it. I would walk all the way around and out the other corridor.

He still didn't speak, but brought his chin up and met my eyes. "I hate him," I thought. But what I said was, "I'm so sorry."

"Wait," he said as I shoved by him out the door. In turning so abruptly, my shoulder rubbed across his chest and my knee brushed his pants leg. "That monster," I thought. I should have hit him, strangled him. I imagined telling Daniel about the asshole who kept bothering me. The little bit of watch band had kept his skin from my skin. But the parts of me that had touched his clothes still ruffled, as if my nerves were working to memorize the sensation. I knew even as I rehearsed it that I wouldn't say anything to Daniel. He'd get upset and keep me up all night. I would end up soothing and comforting him, when it was me who needed care. I couldn't go back to my desk, or finish the copying, which was due by three o'clock.

"I'm sick," I told Susanna. "I'm going out for a minute." I rushed outside without my coat. The cold air clawed through my collar. I had no money and no keys. A bus whipped by, puffing black exhaust. Two women chatting stepped around me. A man spoke authoritatively into his phone, not even slowing to negotiate, "Six? No seven, seven."

I got to the corner as the streetlight blinked red. All around me people lunged into the intersection anyway. A cab honked at the couple in front of me. The man slapped its hood and kept on going. No one seemed to notice how loud it was out here, brakes screeching, metal cables slapping flagpoles, heels of dress shoes tapping the pavement, the doors of a delivery van grinding open while the guy at the luggage store leaned in his doorway, disdainfully smoking.

ENHANCED DISTRIBUTION

The Southern Empire's attack came without warning, a massive strike on Marmoral's nascent air force and a march over the border securing several key southern towns. Maybe there had been a letter or proclamation, an ultimatum, but the Marmolian politicians had gotten used to ignoring those. The prime minister was at a hockey game when the news came. The tv footage showed him rising abruptly, his face ashen, but rumors persisted that he had stayed another fifteen minutes because his team was about to score. Seven soldiers died in a gun battle outside the town of Scofield, along with some air mechanics and cleaning women, sandwich cart vendors at the base. I was tempted to say that Marmoral's casualties were light, but as I had dreamed up all these people—a sullen fourteen-year-old who drove his divorced mother's van down the long straight drive to the airbase every evening after school to sweep out the canteen—I had trouble seeing them as numbers.

It was no use my curling into my chair wondering why. I couldn't even take a day off work for the disaster. There I was in the file room, the drawers rolling obediently out on their oiled casters, smearing the documents with my teary fingers.

"You're next," I told Daniel. But the Belgravians were expert negotiators, in fact had multiple talks going on, some official, some back-channel, some secret even from the president. A delegation of Belgravian literati toured the Empire and dedicated a sister city—undoubtedly some pedantic backwater. Belgrave's bad-boy philosopher won a prestigious Imperial prize and spoke to adoring crowds at the colleges and think tanks. As expected, he published a scathing book when he returned—Imperial culture was wrapped in a condom, coated in plastic, deadened. "He's finally lost his sense of play," wrote the reviewers, eager to at last unleash their spite. He grew to hate the cover photo, his sour face peering out of an ostentatiously Belgravian-manufactured car. His mistress enjoyed his trip abroad, and had let herself marry her young lover.

The Imperial troops left Marmoral's capital alone and declared a policy of no harm toward civilians in the captured territory. They only wanted us to buy their rice and wheat and clear a path for a railway, which would make for enhanced distribution. While the prime minister resigned, and half his cabinet, too, his cousin Hugo was more obliging. He signed the treaty, really more of a trade agreement, and Marmoral's forests burped out millions of railroad ties.

"It's okay," I told Daniel. "Their terms aren't so bad. It's humiliating. But they just want us to buy more of their crap."

"Not so bad, then," he said. He came and perched himself on the arm of my big chair. He hadn't come so close to me for months, at least not deliberately. If we brushed by each other in the kitchen, it couldn't be helped. In bed, we each occupied our sides, and only rolled into each other when we were unconscious. Some parts of us, maybe our shoulders, were a bit behind the times, like a liquor store in a small town that produces from its basement club soda from a bottler long ago refitted and absorbed into the dominant brand. But the rest of our bodies followed the new regulations strictly, and any overt settling next to each other had fallen away.

"My poor little monkey," he said, nuzzling my hair. I hadn't felt his lips for a long time, either. Their function had slimmed down, and lately they only pronounced words, or maybe narrowed grimly at me from across the room. They certainly hadn't met my lips, or any other exposed surface. Even through my hair, this bit of warmth and movement was more than I could bear. I clung to him, almost like I used to.

We had spent almost all our time indoors, but once, when we hadn't known each other very long, I made him come for a walk with me. I had something to tell him, which was that I couldn't see him anymore because I didn't think he was kind. I couldn't figure out how to illustrate his unkindness. He should have said and done some things differently, I thought. But that wasn't very clear. So we walked down to the old post office and around back through the tennis court. It was not a good night for a walk, getting cold and eventually starting to drizzle. I lived with my sister's family so I could take care of her four-year-old on the days I didn't work. I had told her I was going out to do an errand and would be back in an hour. She probably knew exactly what I meant. But still the minutes ticked on until the time I'd said I'd be back. So we ended up outside my door again, wet and shivering, and neither of us had said anything the whole time. But I had nevertheless stopped thinking he was unkind, and when we kissed fervently until someone came to the window, it seemed we had reached an agreement.

I let him go almost at the same time as he slid off the chair, saying he had something to do. Even the back of his neck seemed to me crafty, the way it was so elevated with the springiness of his walk. "Did you have plans?" I called after him. He answered with a sound, not a yes or a no, as he vanished through the kitchen. It might have been better to ask for everything in writing, I thought. I could say it wasn't in my nature to demand that things be more clearly spelled out. But even I could see that "nature" wasn't what was involved here. Again and again I failed to protect myself. The television consoled me for a little while, until the news came on—markets in turmoil, secret weapons lab suspected, wildfires, robberies, a church burned. Daniel stayed busy in the other room. I kept myself from going to bed until I was sure he was sound asleep.

FERTILITY

Marmoral's dissidents plastered the capital with a photo of me and Daniel. A friend had snapped it from across the street as we approached his house for drinks and a game of cards. Our friend had taken another photo that same evening, of me laughing against Daniel's shoulder, but that one Daniel had ripped up, in anger or by accident, depending on your perspective. The remaining photo of the two of us showed us walking arm in arm, but because my hair had gotten trapped in his cuff buttons, my head was jerked back, and I was straining my neck awkwardly. It had been such a pleasant evening, with friends who had since moved to the farthest suburbs so we could rarely afford the train fare. Yet the picture showed a prisoner propelled, in pain, against her will. It worried me that Daniel could look so coercive, and I would have destroyed this photo when he wrecked the happier one except that he looked so handsome in his winter coat and my face particularly luminous.

The slogans underneath the image were simple: villain, traitor, tyrant. They blamed me, and blamed him, for what was happening to our sacred mountain. The railroad charged up the slope, racketing over villages on immense steel stanchions. The Imperial engineers sank these enormous limbs deep into the ground to withstand the ranges of temperature and threat of earthquake. Instead of moseying around the slope, the tracks hastened up the most direct route, bridging gorges and rivers. It didn't care what it trod over, and everywhere beneath and around the tracks piled sand, ash, broken rock and debris. Soon a vast, white-tiled department store squashed into a ravine not far from the summit. The villagers came to shop, marveling at the hauture of the Imperial goods—gauzy halter tops, denim shorts, push-up bras, and shelves of neat plastic strainers, toilet brushes, frying pans, curtain rings. Under the brrrrrng of the cash registers they could barely hear the chant of the drills sending the first tunnels down into the virgin copper mines.

Marmolians protested. The traditional buildings had been designed to harmonize with the spiritual world. The holiday hotels pranced on ash poles, biting only lightly into the sacred ground. The direction of the door of every tea hut had been researched and sanctified by the mountain monks. Even pissing and washing your hands was a holy act on the mountaintop, even spitting into a spittoon. The direction and flow of every human action had been aligned with channels of energy pouring off the peak. Women wanting to conceive on their August visit followed diagrams woven into the coverlet showing where their heads should rest and where their heels, in order to be most open to the fertile winds of the universe.

"Spread your legs," Daniel said to me the very first time we'd made love, in a borrowed apartment, the real tenant due back in less than an hour. My legs were already open, he was inside me already, but his commanding me opened something else up, an interior dissolve that made me gasp and dig my fingers into his hips. I had acquiesced to him, though what we were doing had a moment before seemed entirely and urgently mutual. "Let me in," he said, thrusting harder. I was only dimly aware at that point of how much farther in there was to me, to both of us, and what I would do to get away, to keep him out.

FIRE IV – ASHES

Time was going so quickly—it was already November, almost December there, the months raging headlong, while we were still picking our feet through late September. The cold wind rushed down the mountain. Mud clogged the sewers, then dried in ribbons over the grates. The kids went out at sundown to collect wood for the bonfires, weaseling home long after dark, having ranged through several neighborhoods where they were forbidden to go. Migratory birds came down the river, soiling the developments in the lowlands—it happened the same way every year. Aach! Wipe your feet! Don't come in the house that way! But how close it was still, almost just at the end of the street, maybe the end of the bed: the sun, summer, heatstroke, the blazing headache you got when you came in after lying in the chair in the garden all afternoon.

Nevertheless Sunday stretched on forever, tearing us into shreds. First, Daniel was in one room and I was in the other. Then he came in looking for the mesh for the putty, and I retreated to the bedroom. Then he was back, worrying at the cracks, and I drifted to the kitchen, where there was nothing to eat. Our paths crossed and tangled, a knotted invisible weaving that even so could not be dissolved by our not touching.

The bad-boy philosopher looked out the window and wrote this down in his notebook: *past the rooftops of the apartments below, tiles crumbling on the grocery across the way, telephone lines, way away one street over, a woman in a pink blouse leans out the window yelling something to someone below. Then she's quiet, her mouth not moving, and she brings her fist to her cheek.* But he'd made it all up. He went on to describe her chin, her lips, her absolute vivaciousness. It was only what he'd like to have seen, had he still lived in his old rental in the Third Quarter. He's moved now to a nice new villa, and his new girlfriend is even prettier than his old one. But every day, as soon as he wakes up, his own worthlessness stabs him in the stomach.

The Southern Empire, with all its riches, persuaded one of the fire priests to come to the capital and perform his ritual in the stadium. None of the top holy men would go, but even a level-three priest, a regional father, provided a worthy spectacle. From a refrigerated capsule he produced copious sweat, which the camera magnified for the big screen, the droplets struggling Olympianly down his arms. Then he dried himself from within by kindling his bones, and steam swaddled him. A parade of women with stupendous breasts arched backwards, offering their sternums as tabletops. The priest placed an enchanted candle on each of their proffered planes, and lit them one by one by passing his hand over the wicks. The people in their seats sighed "aahhhh…" as the last flame leapt up under his palm and the light sparkled off the beauties' lacquered nipples. Yet all the audience's combined exhalations were not enough to blow the candles out.

What if I lost all the detail, and could only tell you about things in a general sense? All the edges had turned a little metallic—or was it just ashy?—slightly silvery, a kind of ghostly powder, hard but not exactly bright. There was still something there, lumped into sacklike nouns, a little adjectival sprinkle sifting out of the open seams. It was like a skeleton, like a burned forest filled still with the uprightness of the former trees, their spacing maintained by their crusted stumps, leafiness and liveliness now only inferred from the gray material so consistently covering the charcoaled ground. There's still a little bit there, the last big protest march still to come, when the priests will soak the parishioners' fingers in mutton fat and ignite them and they'll stream down the mountain together, the fire cult with its thousand little lights, demanding to hold onto their heritage.

But beyond that, the sound of the protesters' ribs cracking beneath the soldiers' boots, the bullets whining out of the mass-produced aluminum rifles, the pink smear of blood and sheep grease pooling downhill, the squawk of a sandpiper running away from the trash pickers in the train yard—well, that's what I'm telling you slid away, is even now sliding. You could call it nacreous, or perhaps, inaccurately, cartilaginous, but not fleshly, not the exact ringing detail—a substance glowing like soap, dense, dull, opalescent. That's all I'm left with.

"Come out with me," I said, and he got his coat. Daniel, I would have said, how dreadful to be so attuned. The sound of his boots rasping through the fallen leaves scraped at me, its contrast to my softer crunch seeming so inevitable, that we lived in different registers. My eyes, cast down, caught all the candy wrappers and abandoned socks, the expired bus tickets and spent burger wrappers, while he, six inches taller and looking resolutely into the distance, recorded the warning hands of the streetlights and the fleeing beams of truck brakes.

INSOMNIA

The new government forbade me to enter Marmoral. A short letter thanked me for past services and conveyed every kind of warmth and honor. Nowhere did it say that I was to keep away. I understood, though, that this was how it was done. When I huddled in my chair and tried to imagine my country, now briskly expanding the airports, throwing up more workmen's shacks along the railroad lines, pouring concrete for the multiplying Imperial superstores, all I saw was a fuzzy grayness. This mist hung in front of me wherever I went.

At work, Susanna hung up the phone on her mother like she always did—"I get it, Mom, okay, okay!"—and plucked at me as I walked past. One of the partners had asked her to type and proofread his daughter's high school history project.

"Can you believe it?" she said, waving the notebook paper embossed in girly pencil. For an instant the red of Susanna's sweater struck at me, and I recalled what I would have said in happier times. We would have dined out on this brash request for weeks. Susanna hadn't said she couldn't do it, but asked him if he would like her to get to it before she started the quarterly report, for which he still hadn't turned in his figures.

"His face went scarlet!" she said. She began to intone some choice phrases from the daughter's essay. I hurried back to the file room, where a sheaf of documents drowsed in the in-tray.

I propped myself up in bed reading a mystery. It seemed the old man might have switched his medications himself, just to make it look like his wife had poisoned him. But why was his sister-in-law fleeing in the Bentley? Daniel hated the lamp shining on his face. "In a minute," I said when he complained. I swooned in front of the page, the story pausing politely while my head nodded. But as soon as I turned out the light and lay down, I popped back awake.

If I pretend to sleep, I'll sleep, I thought. I closed my eyes, breathed evenly and deeply, taking every now and then a little gulping swallow. But this was just the outward shape of sleep. I needed real sleep to seep over my tongue, spread out inside me, slip its fingers through tight cuffs, my wrists. I'll let it wear me like a coat, I promised. Sleep can abduct me, pull me by the ankles. My head will bounce along the pavement, and the whole night sky can rake its claws over me. But still I lay awake. Sleep sat primly in the straight-backed chair in the corner and didn't even look at me.

QUIET

Daniel got an evening job doing a little cleaning and maintenance at the school. Sometimes when we were both at home, the air pressed into the floor, leaving up by the ceiling a thin, empty atmosphere. I would have liked to go up there, hang upside down, the rug a distant pasture, the coat hooks and electrical sockets all wrongly placed. Now the apartment was peaceful, though not quiet. The refrigerator hummed remorselessly. No human voice, but the mechanical vibration filled the kitchen, overflowed into the living room, and finally met the clock whirring by the bed.

Then the train bullied its way in. The tracks are a mile off, the streets don't go through, you can't even get near—but the sound of its horn, the churning wheels, sped right in the little gaps under the windows. The train brought the whole evening with it, a car rattling into the neighbor's drive, the woman upstairs dragging something across the floor. The sounds sat down, needed to be offered drinks. Can I put my feet on this? It was so jolly, though they mostly talked among themselves.

Summer here is so loud no one can sleep. The whole neighborhood is up all night because the nineteen-year-olds are drinking on the stoops, blasting their dance mixes. Car alarms shriek—blowing leaves are enough to set them off. A woman screams out the window, "I'll tell you what! I'll tell you what you can do!" A low voice answers from somewhere below, "Tell me about it. Just tell me." We can't help hearing, but we aren't getting the story clearly. Why doesn't she just tell him already, so we know what happened?

I went out to get some milk, though when I got to the corner, I didn't turn towards the market. I passed by my sister's, but I didn't go in there either. A hole in one glove let in the frost, even with my hands clenched in my pockets. If I walked by the school, there was a chance that I'd see Daniel waltzing a stepladder around. He wouldn't be whistling, but he'd have that happy tilt of the head, like a circus hand in an old movie idly, competently rearranging the props just before the fatal fire breaks out. If Daniel were to look out the undraped school windows as I walked by, he wouldn't see me. The light was all on the inside. But I didn't go that way, anyway, but over to the park and the hospital. This particular park was considered safe even at night because the attendants in the parking lot and helicopter pad kept an eye on it from their secure boxes.

I wondered if I might glimpse the man-moth climbing an old oak. I had been about to set him loose in Marmoral—a gigantic night creature with ghostly green wings. Maybe he was only a legendary monster, a seducer of young brides. They would have outgrown him by now. They had no time for the man-moth in Marmoral, now they were getting used to the scientific management of the new regime. Probably a long time ago fathers had warned their daughters not to show off their charms. If he caught her sitting in her nightie in the window, combing out her long black hair, he'd say, "The man-moth will come. His wings are beautiful, but think of his little prickly feet!"

I skirted the helicopter pad, which was ringed with signs on posts saying not to walk on it. Canister lights glazed a bright X across it. Despite the dark and cold, a couple of women lounged against the benches, babies bundled into strollers, toddlers careening on the little merry-go-round. Solitary figures trailed after their dogs. Maybe it wasn't nearly as late as I'd thought it was.

A man with a little furry thing on a leash sat down near me. "That's a Pomeranian, isn't it?" I said. I had learned all the dog breeds from a book when I was eight. But I was wrong. It was a Chihuahua, the long-haired kind. "Very similar, though, I think," he said. It wasn't his dog, but belonged to his girlfriend's mother, who was too ill to take it out now. She was in the hospital right over there, as a matter of fact. I wondered if the old woman could see her dog out the window. But he said he thought her room was on the other side. In any case, she was so sick she could barely turn her head.

"But we've got our health," he said. I supposed later that "we" must have meant him and his girlfriend. But I took it to mean both of us, sitting out in the dark, enjoying the crisp near-winter air. We'd both been cooped up all day, me in the office doing my filing and copying, him somewhere else, maybe supervising deliveries at a drug store. All our muscles and bones were in place, our lungs pumping, hearts sucking in blood. No need for antibiotics to drip into us through a tube in the hand. We didn't have to force our lids open to squint at a nurse's hard face. How marvelous.

When I got home, the sounds had let themselves out. I cleaned up the mess they'd made, rings on the coffee table, crumbs on the floor. The window rattled a little bit. But it was just saying goodbye. Yes, it was very quiet. My footsteps hardly made a noise, and left no impressions behind them on the floor. The sheets sighed, barely audible, as I turned them back. The switch on the bedside lamp coughed once, then said nothing more. An entire day, in fact months and years, rushed away down their sewer with only a gentle rustle.

SILVER LAKE

"What's going on in Belgrave?" I asked my husband. He had softened towards me a little bit. I thought I was putting a good face on things, but still, he'd said he didn't like to see me so sad. Once we'd even—but no, it didn't mean anything, did it? Just animals mating, because we were used to it. It wasn't enough to change the new order.

"I can tell you about a scientist who took his family on a picnic," he said.

But I couldn't bear it. I already knew what that would be like. Though he clearly meant it kindly, I did not want to imagine the hampers of cold chicken and deviled eggs, the children's sandy feet shedding grit all over the blankets, this scientist, whoever he was, laying his head in his wife's lap and falling into the most stirring and scientifically useful dream—the rotation of the motor he hadn't been able to figure out suddenly whirring before him, the formula that eliminated friction appearing in his mind as a distant cityscape, resolving into an orderly set of numbers. The wind blew across the reeds. The children's shouts carried through the rushes, but the mother could no longer see them. She hoped they hadn't gone too deep. She worried that leeches would sink their jaws into her daughter's calves, that crayfish would pinch the little one's toes. Her husband moved his lips in his sleep. What was he saying? Hadn't she at one point wanted to marry someone else? But this man, the scientist, had surprised her by beseeching her—"But I need you!" She'd had no idea she could hurt him. He seemed so self-contained. So she'd given in. And how wonderfully it had all worked out.

"No thank you," I said. "I just thought there might be some news."

He had the pile of bills in one hand. In the other, the checkbook flopped. He sat down at the table and set to. There must have been something I should have been doing, too, but I didn't know what it was.

I went into the kitchen, and now I was behind him, behind his bent and studious back. I watched his shoulder move, his whole arm engaged even in minute motions of the pen. Tiny geological upheavals played themselves out as the wrinkles in his shirt straightened and reformed. It should have been so easy to fold myself over him. He must have longed for that as much as I did, our former comfortable, unspoken physicality. But a whole lake opened up between the kitchen counter and Daniel's chair. My feet sank into the gooey, sandy bottom. Minnows streamed around my legs, and from somewhere nearby rose the stench of a dead carp, ripe and beastly in the late afternoon air. Soon gnats and mosquitoes and black flies would make it unbearable, but right now it was possible to stand quietly and watch the sun flash across the surface of the water. The waves lapped Daniel's ankles while he went on with his borrowing and carrying.

"Look," I wanted to say. I could see under the water, the weeds undulating, green beards wavering off sunken rocks, slimed sticks jutting out of the ooze, the open jaws of dead mussels. Olive and brown strands of detritus thickened the chilly depths. A dark shadow may have been the opening of an algae-laden cave. Perhaps this was my future dwelling place, a watery crevice, where I would be the sole member of my civilization.

At the same time the whole top of the lake stretched out like a silver hand. Even now, at what was surely a late date, an era of decline, a landscape offered itself to us. Way in the distance may have been our sacred mountain, still, despite the egregious terms, under our joint ownership. In fact the summit, upside down, threw its reflection towards us, fragmenting with the waves, shimmering, not quite holding together.

"Daniel," I said. "Darling."

"What?" he said, not turning to me.

Even though he didn't see it, I found the water beautiful.

Angela Woodward is the author of "The Human Mind."
She lives in Madison, Wisconsin.